How PRUDENCE PROOVIT

Proved the Truth About Fairy Tales

by Coleen Murtagh Paratore

illustrated by Tamara Petrosino

SIMON & SCHUSTER BOOKS FOR YOUNG READERS

New York   London   Toronto   Sydney   Singapore

Once there was a girl who didn't believe in fairy tales. If Prudence Proovit couldn't prove it, well, it just wasn't so.

Prudence's parents, the professors, tutored her from dawn to dusk in their big stone house on the hill. Declaring nursery rhymes for ninnies and fairy tales for fools, the professors filled Prudence with facts: Tests at teatime. Dictionaries at dinner.

Alone in Tutor Tower, Prudence wished for

curly hair,

a dollhouse,

and most of all, a sister.

But alas, Prudence's wishes
never came true.

Prudence was the smartest girl in Lilliville. And the most unhappy. She watched children laughing at the bus stop below and longed for Saturdays when she'd be set free, from two until three, to play with Suzy Wiffle.

Then one day, pleased with Prudence's progress, the professors announced an experiment.

School.

A real school with a real teacher, with my best friend,
Suzy Wiffle. Prudence was overjoyed.

Until the mail arrived.

The professors rolled their eyes but agreed to give school
a try.

Prudence wrote back: "Please, not that Snow White stuff! How about science instead?" Later Prudence told Suzy a well-known fact: "Fairy tales are for featherbrains, and I'll prove it."

Now, Suzy loved fairy tales, but Prue knew everything, so Suzy spread the word to Lexy Ray.

And Prudence got another postcard:

Hi-Ho, Prudo,
You sure aren't bashful.
Why so grumpy? Are
you sleepy?
Happy wishes,
S. W. and the D's

S. W.? Suzy Wiffle?
Prudence was amused.

On Opening Day, Miss Bliss blew in and read *Hansel and Gretel* with gusto. "And here's the clue for tomorrow! Who barged in for breakfast and broke the furniture?"

"Here's another clue," Prudence began proving. "Who's the original dumb blonde? Did you guess Goldilocks? *Ding, ding, ding!*" Some kids laughed.

Suzy and Lexy looked sad.

Dear Prunella,
Sorry about your hair, but
don't blame blondes.
Having more fun as
always,
Goldie and the B's

Even though she was insulted, Prudence complimented Suzy on her clever writing.

"Thanks, Prue," Suzy said, "but I don't know what you're talking about."

Then who's been sending the postcards?

Prudence proved on the playground. "See any problems with *glass* slippers? Ever tried climbing a *bean plant*?"

Miss Bliss approached her kindly. "Fairy tales are good, Prue. A bit of believing makes wishes come true."

Prudence remembered the curly hair, dollhouse, and sister. "Wishes never worked for me, Miss Bliss."

"Maybe you forgot the believing part, Prue. A bit of that might work for you."

But when Miss Bliss read Riding Hood, Prudence grimaced over Granny.

"And couldn't that girl tell a woman from a wolf? Were her brains in that basket too?"

Everyone giggled. But Suzy seemed sorry for Miss Bliss.

Listen, Prudence,
I'm red. My brothers
are grim. Please forgo
this fairy-tale feud.
L. R. Hood

L. R.? Lexy Ray? Prudence was puzzled. She wished she could prove who was sending these postcards.

Armed with buttons and banners, Prudence protested in the cafeteria. "Okay. Show your forks! Who's seen a frog in a crown? Pigs in construction hats? And excuse the bare fact, but couldn't that naked emperor feel a breeze?"

Dear Prude,
Lighten up. I know about tower life. It helps to let down your hair.

"R."

"R." for Ray? Lexy doesn't have a tower. Should I consult the professors? No. They might end the experiment. And school is such fun!

The next day Miss Bliss bubbled with news.

"A Costume Ball Breakfast. Our fairy-tale finale. You bring families. I'll bring goodies!"

The class cheered. Suzy and Lexy passed notes about costumes.

Prudence pranced forward. "May I recite a poem?"

"Why certainly, dear."

"Fairy tales are stupid, fairy tales are dumb; if you believe in fairy tales, your brain must be a plum."

Miss Bliss gasped. Nobody laughed.

Suzy and Lexy whispered on the bus like best friends. Prudence felt lonelier than she ever had in Tutor Tower. Sure enough, she had mail.

Little Miss Proovit,
Quit huffing and
puffing. You're being
a ham.
Big B. W. and the Oinks

Big B. W.? Prudence was perplexed. She needed mightier minds.

The professors paled at the postcards, then reddened with rage. "That school is for simpletons!"

And then when Prudence dropped the Ball gently, the professors proclaimed it "hair-brained as Halloween."

But seeing their daughter's dismay, they commenced costume research.

Prudence cried herself to sleep. *I've lost Suzy, hurt Miss Bliss, the professors are ending the experiment, and someone's sending me postcards. All over fairy tales? I wish I could . . . I wish I could . . . I wish I could BELIEVE!*

In the morning a costume was waiting. There was a card on the windowsill.

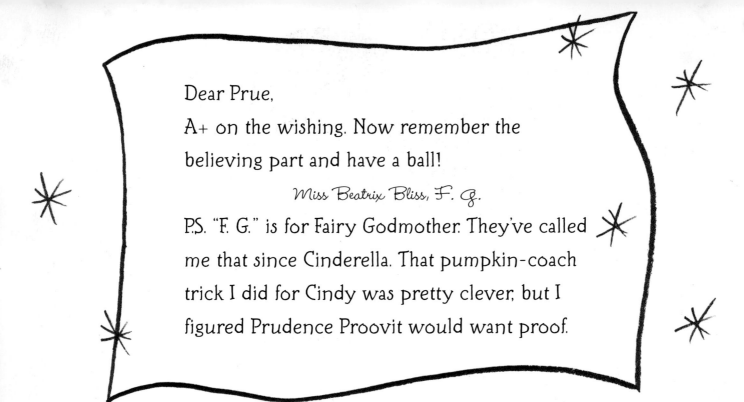

Dear Prue,

A+ on the wishing. Now remember the believing part and have a ball!

Miss Beatrix Bliss, F. G.

P.S. "F. G." is for Fairy Godmother. They've called me that since Cinderella. That pumpkin-coach trick I did for Cindy was pretty clever, but I figured Prudence Proovit would want proof.

F. G. stands for Fairy Godmother, of course! And S. W. is for Snow White. . . . Finally it all made sense!

Prudence laughed so hard, her hair curled.

Everyone stared as the Proovits entered the Ball.

"You said fairy tales were dumb," Suzy snapped.

"Fairy tales are real," Prudence pleaded.

"Then prove it," Lexy demanded.

The crowd circled. Could Prudence prove it?

Think. Prudence closed her eyes. *Think*.

"That's right, dear," Miss Bliss whispered. "It's good to think. And to wish.

"Now, just *BELIEVE*."

Prudence heard her heart thump. *Be-lieve, be-lieve, be-lieve . . .*

"You have all you need now, dear. The proof is in your pocket!"

Prudence opened her eyes. There was Suzy with fingers crossed. The professors, proud as peacocks. The people Prudence Proovit loved, well, they believed in her too. So without a single doubt, she reached in her pocket and pulled something out.

The postcards.

The people of Lilliville oohed and ogled and argued like professors. In the end they agreed. Fairy tales must be true because Prudence had mail postmarked "Fairy Tale Forest"! Cheers rose and rained like confetti on the girl who reigned at the Ball. Prudence Proovit had proven the truth about fairy tales, indeed.

Miss Bliss winked. "You are a prodigy, Prue."
The professors wept. "What a brilliant school!"
Suzy said, "Prue, you rule," and they went off
for goodies, best friends again.

After the Ball Miss Bliss bid farewell; another town
needed her now.

Sadly Prue's new curls drooped straight. The dollhouse
never came. But Prudence kept on believing. Finally,
one day, her greatest wish came true.

And while the professors dance in the tower each night
like perfect ninnies and fools, Prudence Proovit is
teaching her new baby sister the truth about fairy tales.

With thanks to:
Tony, who trusted,
Chris, Connor, and Dylan, who wished,
Noreen, who nurtured,
Alyssa, who believed,
and my mother, Peg Spain Murtagh,
for the kind of love that makes fairy tales come true.
—C. M. P.

To Lisa, Meredith, Stephanie, Pearl, Sabine, Laura,
and the rest of my friends and family who believed in me.
With love
—T. P.

SIMON & SCHUSTER BOOKS FOR YOUNG READERS

An imprint of Simon & Schuster Children's Publishing Division
1230 Avenue of the Americas, New York, New York 10020
Text copyright © 2004 by Coleen Murtagh Paratore
Illustrations copyright © 2004 by Tamara Petrosino
All rights reserved, including the right of reproduction in whole or in part in any form.
SIMON & SCHUSTER BOOKS FOR YOUNG READERS is a trademark of Simon & Schuster, Inc.
Book design by Mark Siegel
The text for this book is set in Bodoni and Pink Flamingo.
The illustrations for this book are rendered in brush and ink,
colored pencils, and watercolor on Arches cold press watercolor paper.
Manufactured in China
2 4 6 8 10 9 7 5 3 1
CIP data for this book is available from the Library of Congress.
ISBN 0-689-86274-1